The Berenstain Bears®

W9-CFU-900

"The season of singing has come."
—Song of Songs 2:12

ZONDERKIDZ

The Berenstain Bears® Go Christmas Caroling
Copyright © 2019 by Berenstain Publishing, Inc.
Illustrations © 2019 by Berenstain Publishing, Inc.

Requests for information
should be addressed to:
Zonderkidz, 3900 *Sparks Dr. SE,*
Grand Rapids, Michigan 49546
Custom ISBN 978-0-310-63313-6

Library of Congress Cataloging-in-Publication Data
Names: Berenstain, Mike, 1951-author, illustrator.
Title: The Berenstain Bears go Christmas caroling / by Mike Berenstain.
Description: Grand Rapids, Michigan: Zonderkidz, [2019] | Summary: After a
    sleigh ride with Farmer Ben, the entire Berenstain Bear family joins the
    Bear Country Carolers for a round of Christmas Eve celebrations with
    their Neighbors and friends. Includes a word search puzzle. |
Identifiers: LCCN 2019007024 (print) | LCCN 2019010224 (ebook) | ISBN
    9780310763659 () | ISBN 9780310763635 (saddle stitch)
Subjects; | CYAC: Caroling—Fiction. | Christmas—Songs and music—Fiction. |
    Neighbors—Fiction. | Bears—Fiction.
Classification: LCC PZ7.B44827 (ebook) | LCC PZ7.B44827 Bfr 2019 (print) |
DDC [E]—dc23
LC record available at https://lccn.loc.gov/2019007024

Editor: Annette Bourland
Design: Cindy Davis

Printed in China

22 23 24 25 26 27 28 29 / DSC / 12 11 10 9 8 7 6 5 4

By Mike Berenstain
Based on the characters created by
Stan & Jan Berenstain

Living Lights™
A Faith Story

ZONDERkidz

It was Christmas Eve deep in Bear Country and the whole Bear family was busy turning their tree house home into one big Christmas tree. Papa was up on a ladder stringing colored lights. Mama was hanging holly wreaths. Sister, Brother, and Honey were tying red bows to the mailbox, while Grizzly Gramps and Gran wrapped evergreen garland around the fence.

Gran cast a critical eye on the tree.

"Too much red up top, Sonny," she called to Papa. Papa shrugged and shifted some red lights down. He knew better than to argue with Gran. Then, into the lights' warm glow, a single white flake came drifting down.

"Look!" said Sister. "It's beginning to snow."

Sure enough, more and more flakes were dancing through the air.
"Looks like it's going to be a white Christmas," said Gramps.
"Just like the ones we used to know!" agreed Gran.

Now, the snow came thick and fast. The ground was soon covered. The sound of sleigh bells came through the snow. It was Farmer Ben in his one-horse sleigh.

"Merry Christmas!" he called. "It's a perfect night for a sleigh ride. Would you care to join me?"

The Bear family needed no coaxing.

"Giddap, Bess!" Ben called to his horse and they were off, jingling merrily on their way.

"How about a round of 'Jingle Bells?'" suggested Ben. They all joined in.

"Jingle bells! Jingle bells! Jingle all the way!
 Oh, what fun it is to ride in a one-horse open sleigh!
 Bells on bob tails ring, making spirits bright.
 What fun it is to laugh and sing a sleighing song tonight!"

"Farmer Ben," said Sister, "what are bells on *bob tails*?"

Ben pointed to his horse. "See how I've trimmed Bess' tail? That's called bobbing. When she swishes her tail, the bells make a merry sound!"

As they drove through the night, an even merrier sound was heard—Christmas carols being joyfully sung.

"That's the Bear Country Carolers," said Ben. "They're out on their Christmas Eve rounds singing from home to home. Greetings, neighbors!"

"Merry Christmas!" the group called back.

"Look!" said the cubs. "There's Cousin Fred. Hiya, Fred!"

"Come and join us!" called Fred.

"You folks go ahead," said Farmer Ben as the Bear family climbed down. "I'm heading back to the farm. Mrs. Ben and I have chores to do. See you when you get there!" He drove off in a jingle of bells.

"What are you singing next?" Gramps asked the carolers.

"Let's see …" said their leader, leafing through his songbook.

"My favorite is, 'Good King Wenceslas,'" said Gramps, and he began to sing loudly.

"Gramps," said Sister, "who was King Wenceslas and why was he looking at Stephen's feet?"

"That's *feast of Stephen*, not *feet*!" laughed Gramps. "King Wenceslas was a king, you see … and the Feast of Stephen was, well …"

Cousin Fred, who read the dictionary for fun, spoke up. "Wenceslas was a king of Bohemia who took care of the poor and needy. The Feast of Stephen was …"

But he was drowned out when the carolers started to sing again.

We wish you a merry Christmas!
We wish you a merry Christmas!
We wish you a merry Christmas!
And a happy New Year!

They arrived at a large and impressive house. This was the home of Squire and Lady Grizzly who came out on the front steps to listen to the carolers.

"We all want some figgy pudding!
We all want some figgy pudding!
We all want some figgy pudding!
So, bring some right here!"

Honey wasn't sure what "figgy" pudding was. But she knew she liked pudding.

"Right here!" she shouted.

Squire and Lady Grizzly laughed and invited them in for refreshments.

Squire Grizzly did, indeed, serve Christmas pudding. But it was honey-flavored not "figgy." Lady Grizzly put finishing touches on her holly wreaths while the carolers struck up a song for the occasion.

"Deck the halls with boughs of holly,
Fa la la la laah, la la la laah!
See the blazing Yule before us,
Fa la la la laah, la la la laah!"

"Lady Grizzly," asked Sister, "what's a *yule* and why is it blazing?"

"That's an old word for a Christmas log, my dear," explained Lady Grizzly, pointing to the fireplace.

There, a stout log was merrily ablaze. Gratefully, the carolers warmed their hands … and other parts.

Now thoroughly heated, the carolers made their way to Farmer Ben's farm. Ben and his wife were in the barn feeding their animals a Christmas Eve dinner. It looked so much like the scene of Jesus's birth in the stable at Bethlehem that the carolers sang,

Away in a manger, no crib for his bed,
The little Lord Jesus laid down his sweet head.
The cattle are lowing. The poor baby wakes.
But little Lord Jesus, no crying he makes.

"Farmer Ben," asked Sister, "what's *lowing*?"
Just then, Farmer Ben's old cow, Bossie, let out a long, loud moo.
"Thanks, Bossie!" laughed Ben. "That's lowing!"

Waving goodbye to Farmer and Mrs. Ben, the carolers moved on to their final stop—the Chapel in the Woods. They were welcomed by Preacher and Mrs. Brown who had hot chocolate ready for them. They gathered around the Chapel's outdoor Christmas scene as they sipped their steaming cups. Then it was time for Christmas Eve services.

The Chapel was warmly lit with
the glow of many candles. As they
filed in, the carolers sang,

"O come, all ye faithful,
Joyful and triumphant,
O come ye, o come ye
To Bethlehem."